SIMON AND SCHUSTER

SIMON AND SCHUSTER
First published in Great Britain in 2013 by Simon and Schuster UK Ltd
1st Floor, 222 Gray's Inn Road, London WC1X 8HB
A CBS Company

Based on the television series Mike the Knight
© 2013 HiT (MTK) Limited/Nelvana Limited. A United Kingdom-Canada Co-production.

ISBN 978-1-4711-2000-8
Printed and bound in China
10 9 8 7 6 5 4 3 2 1
www.simonandschuster.co.uk

Mike THE KNIGHT

and the Great Gallop

Great Gallop Day
comes once a year,
when flowers bloom
and spring is here.
Mike has to be both
brave and strong
so the Vikings
won't stay for long.

Great knights are always great gallopers.

"Wow!" said Squirt. "You and Galahad are so fast!"

"Thanks," replied Mike. "We're going to be running a lot today. It's Great Gallop Day!"

"Oh, I love the sound of the villagers cheering on Great Gallop Day," said Sparkie.

"Today is fantastic," declared Mike, "especially when Dad gallops to the river with a sack of tarts. But he's not here this year, so I wonder who will do it?"

Just then the Queen called Mike and the dragons into the castle. "Mrs Piecrust is baking lots of jam tarts so there'll be plenty to eat and to take down to the river."

"Terrific! But who will do the Great Gallop today?" asked Mike.

"Well…I thought you could, Mike!" said his mum.

"By the King's crown, that's it!
I'm Mike the Knight and my mission
is to be a really fast Great Galloper!"

Mike raced to his
bedroom and pulled the
secret lever to get into his armour.

Mike drew his enchanted sword
to reveal a giant jam tart!

Squirt looked puzzled. "Mike, why do we have to take a sack of tarts to the river?"

"It's just part of the Great Gallop Day tradition," answered Mike. "The important thing is that I gallop as fast as I can!"

And he raced off to Mrs Piecrust's bakery.

In front of the bakery were raspberry tarts, blueberry tarts and gooseberry tarts.

"Wow, they look delicious. Can I take them now so we can start right away?"

"Of course, Mike," said Mrs Piecrust. "Good luck!"

The Town Crier rang his bell to gather everyone round.

"Hear ye, hear ye! The Great Gallop is about to begin! And when it's done we can eat our jam tarts!"

"I can't wait. Yummy!" said Sparkie.

"If Mike the Knight returns before the sand runs out, this will be the fastest Great Gallop **ever**!" the Town Crier said as the Blacksmith turned the giant timer.

"Huzzah! Huzzah!" called the villagers.

"To the river, Galahad!" yelled Mike as he charged
out of the village carrying the giant sack of jam tarts.

Sparkie and Squirt chased after them.

"Mike! The tarts!" gasped Squirt. The sack wasn't closed properly and the tarts were falling out. "We have to go back and get them!"

Mike looked back but galloped on. "It'll take too long. Come on!"

Mike arrived at the river's edge, ready to leave the sack of jam tarts, but it was completely empty!

"Oh, no!" gasped Squirt. "What are we going to do?"

Mike thought, "Well, I've brought the sack to the river, haven't I? It's how fast I gallop that matters!"

Squirt looked worried, "What if the tarts were meant for somebody, though?"

But Mike had already started galloping back to the village. Squirt flew after him. As they left the river, a boat appeared…

Mike and the dragons rushed back to the village, and there was still sand in the timer!

"Mike the Knight has completed the Great Gallop even faster than the King! Once again the village has been saved from Vikings," called the Town Crier.

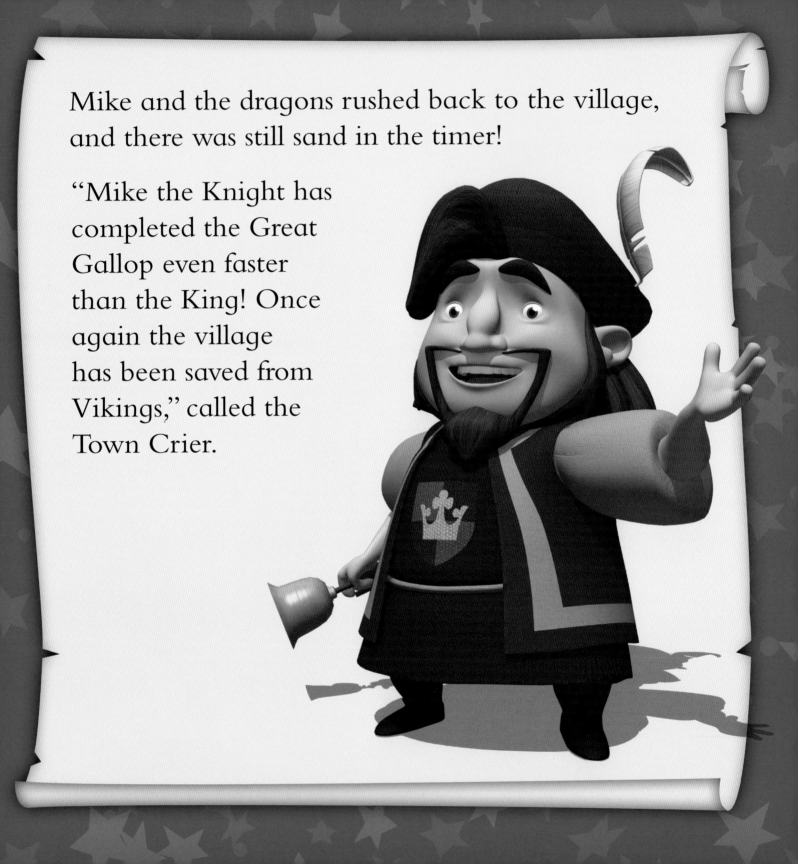

"Err…what's all this about Vikings?" asked Mike.

Evie explained. "When the villagers first made jam tarts, Vikings came and ate them all. So now we leave a sack full of tarts for them to make sure they will leave the village alone!"

"VIKINGS!" Mike, Sparkie and Squirt yelled in unison, as the mischievous trio burst into the village. They had followed the trail of dropped jam tarts.

"Wøaaaaggghhhh! Jøøm tøørt! Jøøm tøørt!" The Vikings bounced around the village, slamming into doors and grabbing the delicious treats.

"Oh no! There are Vikings everywhere and it's all my fault!" cried Mike. "I've got to get them out of here."

He thought hard. "I know! If they like tarts so much, maybe I could lead them away with one.

It's time to be a knight and do it right!"

Mike drew his enchanted sword and waved the giant jam tart at the Vikings. "Sparkie! Squirt! Get the trebuchet!" he yelled.

"Jøøm tøørt! Jøøm tøørt!" chanted the Vikings as they followed Mike through the village.

Mike threw the giant jam tart into the trebuchet's basket and the Vikings plunged in after it.

"Now!" shouted Mike. The dragons released the trebuchet and the Vikings flew through the air away from Glendragon.

Mike grabbed another sack from Mrs Piecrust and fired it after them.

"Huzzah!" cried the villagers.

"Mike the Knight has saved us from the Vikings!" called the Town Crier as the Blacksmith lifted Mike onto his shoulders.

The Queen kissed Mike. "I'm so proud of you," she said.

"And you gave me an idea," said Mrs Piecrust. "When I saw all those different tarts flying through the air I thought of the brand new Viking Mix Tart – strawberry, blueberry and gooseberry – every flavour mixed together!"

"Mmmmm! They're delicious," said Sparkie as he took a big bite. "The best Great Gallop Day tart ever!"

HUZZAH!